For my best friend (aka husband) Shawn and
our three beautiful children, Finn, Roen, and Gwen.
Thank you for bringing an endless warmth
to my heart and to my life.
—KG

For Nyapot and Buom, the ones who melt my heart.
—SH

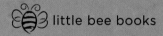 little bee books

New York, NY
Text copyright © 2021 by Kashelle Gourley
Illustrations copyright © 2021 by Skylar Hogan
For information about special discounts on bulk purchases,
please contact Little Bee Books at sales@littlebeebooks.com.
Manufactured in China RRD 0621
First Edition
2 4 6 8 10 9 7 5 3 1
ISBN 978-1-4998-1158-2
littlebeebooks.com

POE and LARS

words by
Kashelle Gourley

pictures by
Skylar Hogan

little bee books

This is Poe.

She lives alone in the Arctic
where it's nice and cold. . . .

Well, mostly.

STOP MELTING!

It gets lonely out here on her own, but she's gained some important life skills. Not to mention the wonders it's done for her imagination.

HELLOOOOOO

HELLOOOOO

Still, some real company would be nice.

Suddenly, Poe felt a rumbling. Then a BANG, BANG, BANG!

Huh?

CRASH!

Poe's home rattled and came tumbling down!

As the snow settled, she saw
a big shadow approach her. . . .

And there he was.

This is Lars.

He also lives alone
in the Arctic.

Lars is big and VERY hangry.

You see . . . he's, uh, not the best hunter.
And food up here is harder and harder to find these days.

He's got a feeling this might be his lucky day, though.

Or . . . maybe not.

Lars had never met such a feisty little creature before.
He decided she wasn't worth his energy.

"HEY! What about my home?!
You can't just leave!
COME BACK!" Poe shouted.

Lars ignored her and
continued walking away,
but then Poe used
the magic word.

FOOD!

"I'll get you food if you rebuild my home!"

And just like that, the deal was struck.

Ok . . . so he's not the best builder, either.

Lars's frustration and hunger continued to grow.

As did his suspicions of Poe. Could she *really* be a better hunter than him?
Something smelled . . .

"Surprised? I'm a girl of my word," Poe said.
"Now, you need to keep yours!"

"CRICK"

"CRICK"

"CRICK"

But all of a sudden . . .

Lars eyed the fish. A glorious feast all to himself?

Maybe it WAS his lucky day.

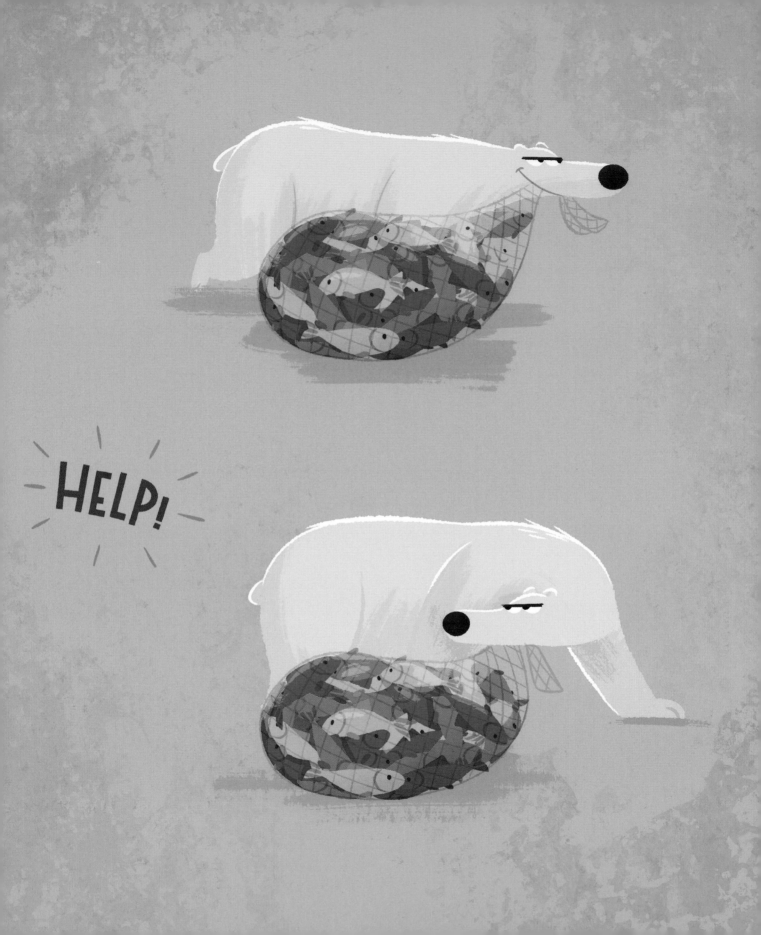

HELP!

Lars thought it over.

The giant polar bear burst out of the water cradling Poe.

"Thank you!" she said.
"For a second, I thought you were going to
take off with the food and just leave me there."

"Well, Fluffy . . .
let's clean this mess up!"

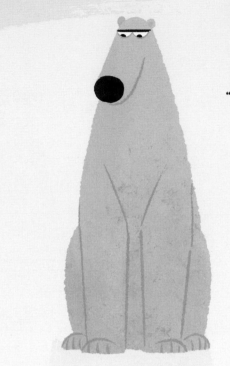

Lars sighed.
"The name's Lars."

Poe's jaw dropped.
"YOU CAN TALK?!"

"Oh, no . . ."

"How old are you?

What's your favorite color?

How much do you weigh?

Are you endangered?

What're your thoughts on the melting ice caps?"

Before they knew it, they were finished rebuilding
Poe's home. Poe marveled at their hard work.
"Can we eat now?" Lars asked.

Together, they feasted by the fire.
Poe, happy to have company.
Lars, happy to have a full belly.

Both feeling a warmth inside their hearts.
A warmth very different from the fire in front
of them. It was a feeling unfamiliar to Lars and . . .

. . . he liked it.

For a second, he had forgotten the
harsh conditions of the Arctic. He thought
maybe it isn't so bad out here after all.

"Nah, life's still rough."

THE ARCTIC AND CLIMATE CHANGE

The Arctic is the northernmost region of the earth and plays an important role in regulating the world's temperature! When Arctic ice melts, the oceans absorb sunlight and heat up, which makes the world warmer. The melting ice also causes sea levels to rise, which can cause flooding. Climate change poses a great danger to the culture and health of the indigenous people living in the Arctic, including the Inuit, Inupiat, Aleut, Yupik, and Chukchi people.

POLAR BEARS

Polar bears live in the Arctic and are the largest carnivores that live on land. A male bear can weigh up to 1,500 pounds! They put on most of their fat for the year between late April to mid-July since the food-free season can last 3 to 4 months. With the rising Arctic temperatures, the ice pack takes more time to form, so bears must wait longer to begin hunting. Their diet consists of seals, whale carcasses, and they occasionally hunt more difficult prey like narwhals and beluga whales.

Did you know that polar bears aren't actually white? Their skin is black, and their hair is hollow with no pigment. When they stand in the sun, all of the light bounces off them, making them look white!